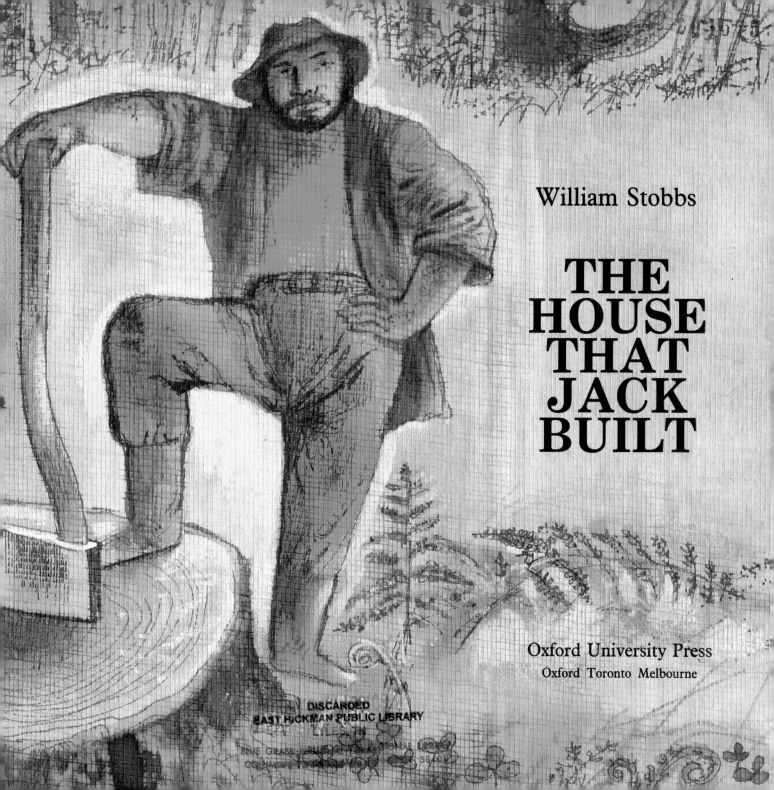

William Stobbs

THE HOUSE THAT JACK BUILT

Oxford University Press

Oxford Toronto Melbourne

This is the house
that Jack built.

This is the malt
That lay in the house
that Jack built.

This is the rat,
That ate the malt
That lay in the house
    that Jack built.

This is the cat,
That killed the rat,
That ate the malt
That lay in the house
        that Jack built.

This is the dog,
That worried the cat,
That killed the rat,
That ate the malt
That lay in the house
    that Jack built.

This is the cow with
    the crumpled horn,
That tossed the dog,
That worried the cat,
That killed the rat,
That ate the malt
That lay in the house
    that Jack built.

This is the maiden
all forlorn,
That milked the cow
with the crumpled horn,
That tossed the dog,
That worried the cat,
That killed the rat,
That ate the malt
That lay in the house
that Jack built.

This is the man all
    tattered and torn,
That kissed the maiden
    all forlorn,
That milked the cow with
    the crumpled horn,
That tossed the dog,
That worried the cat,
That killed the rat,
That ate the malt
That lay in the house
    that Jack built.

This is the priest
   all shaven and shorn,
That married the man
   all tattered and torn,
That kissed the maiden
   all forlorn,
That milked the cow with
   the crumpled horn,
That tossed the dog,
That worried the cat,
That killed the rat,
That ate the malt
That lay in the house
   that Jack built.

This is the cock that
 crowed in the morn,
That waked the priest
 all shaven and shorn,
That married the man
 all tattered and torn,
That kissed the maiden
 all forlorn,
That milked the cow with
 the crumpled horn,
That tossed the dog,
That worried the cat,
That killed the rat,
That ate the malt
That lay in the house
 that Jack built.

This is the farmer sowing his corn,
That kept the cock that crowed in the morn,
That waked the priest all shaven and shorn,
That married the man all tattered and torn,
That kissed the maiden all forlorn,
That milked the cow with the crumpled horn,
That tossed the dog,
That worried the cat,
That killed the rat,
That ate the malt
That lay in the house that Jack built.

This is the horse and the hound and the horn,
That belonged to the farmer sowing his corn,
That kept the cock that crowed in the morn,
That waked the priest all shaven and shorn,
That married the man all tattered and torn,
That kissed the maiden all forlorn,
That milked the cow with the crumpled horn,
That tossed the dog,
That worried the cat,
That killed the rat,
That ate the malt
That lay in the house that Jack built.

E